Catherine Montgomery is the mother of three grown up children. After a 30-year career in medical sales she is now a full time carer living, relatively peacefully, in Scotland.

Apple Crumble is her first published book.

APPLE CRUMBLE

Catherine Montgomery

APPLE CRUMBLE

Nightingale Books

Nightingale Books

© Copyright 2019
Catherine Montgomery
Cover illustration by Hannah Chester

A CIP catalogue record for this title is
available from the British Library.

ISBN 978 1 912021 20 8

Nightingale Books is an imprint of
Pegasus Elliot MacKenzie Publishers Ltd.
www.pegasuspublishers.com

First Published in 2019

Nightingale Books
Sheraton House Castle Park
Cambridge England

Printed & Bound in Great Britain

Acknowledgements

Thank you to Paul Smith for his help and unfailing encouragement. To my children and all their friends who have been an inspiration.

Thank you to Hannah Chester and my daughter, Nathalie, for the lovely illustrations.

For Adam Oyston

Chapter 1

Lenny was deep in twigs, branches, and soft, soggy earth at the bottom of a very, very long garden.

'Lenny, breakfast!' his mum called and into the house he ran with his muddy pyjamas and wet, dirty trainers. Kicking them off, Mum shouted at him.

'Oh Lenny, do go and get washed first, we need to be in school in an hour!'

But the smell of hot buttered toast was too much and on the way to his bedroom Lenny grabbed a finger of toast as he sped by!

It had been a big move. Lenny's father had died in a cycling accident, the family were heartbroken and Lenny's mum decided, after a few months of very deep sadness, to move Lenny and herself from Durham down to London to be near both sets of grandparents and Aunt Minnie. This was hard for Lenny as he had lots of friends at school and in the street where they lived, but he was trying to be brave and wanted to be supportive to his mum so worked hard to help her pack up the house and promised to keep in touch with his mates. Arriving in London was scary and daunting for Lenny, even with his resolve to be tough and strong!

It was Monday morning and he and Mum had been in the flat, which was on the ground floor of an old Victorian house, for just two days. Lenny's room was small, right next to the big kitchen, which made up most of their flat. Mum said that his room would have been the maid's bedroom before the house had been converted into flats, or perhaps a large pantry where people would have kept food fresh before there were fridges. It had a tiny window, very high up on the outside wall so Mum had spent the weekend painting a huge pretend window on the wall with a lovely large beach scene with children making sandcastles!

The little flat was still full of packed boxes with all their things but after tripping over them all weekend, Mum said that she would make a start unpacking while Lenny was at school. His mum loved cleaning and tidying and was always putting his toys and books in places where he couldn't find them!

Chapter 2

Lenny's teacher Miss Gentle, (and she was gentle), smiled a lot and had thick grey hair. She introduced Lenny to the class and then walked over to another boy called Jacob and bringing him out to the front of the class, asked him to show Lenny around the school during the morning break. Jacob was shorter than Lenny but then again most of the children were since Lenny had shot up over the summer according to Mum. Jacob put his hand out to Lenny and gave his hand a big shake.

'I'm going to like this place!' Lenny thought to himself.

Even though everyone was very friendly, his new school felt quite strange and Lenny was pleased when the home-time bell went at three and his mum was waiting at the school gates.

'It was great!' he answered bravely when Mum asked him how his first day had gone.

For tea that evening they had sausages and baked beans. Mum always bought the basics beans as she said you couldn't tell the difference, but Lenny was sure he could! But they were having rice pudding afterwards which he loved. His mum might be great at cleaning but she wasn't a brilliant cook, he thought!

Chapter 3

Next morning when Lenny got up, he went straight down to the bottom of the garden. This time, as he was messing about with the various shrub branches, bending them around and stamping them down and moving stones and twigs to make a small clearing, he noticed a large branch overhanging from the garden next door. He started to pull at it and because he was tall and quite strong for his age, he was just able to reach and bring it down a little so he could make it bounce.

'This looked like fun!' thought Lenny and hoisting himself up he got his arms around the top of the branch and hung in the air for a moment.

Suddenly, looking up the garden towards the house next door he saw a very old, cross face at the window and the face seemed to be shouting! Then a fist banged on the glass very hard. Lenny jumped off the branch and it pinged back into place.

He ran back into the house and screamed loudly, 'Mum, Mum!'

Lenny told her about the face shouting at him.

'Oh Lenny, that must have been the old lady that the estate agent told me about. Her name is Mrs Portman and she doesn't talk to people and doesn't go out much. In fact, nobody knows much about her. You'd better not swing from her branch again!'

Lenny's mum went down to the end of the garden and sure enough the face was still there, peering out through a dirty window from behind old, yellowed curtains.

'Maybe she was too old to keep on top of the housework,' his mum thought.

Then she had a great idea! Running back into the house, Lenny's mum shouted, 'Come and help me. I need your advice! I am going to set up a cleaning company.'

'Wow Mum, you are fantastic at cleaning. That's a brilliant idea!' said Lenny excitedly.

'Thanks Lenny. The Brilliant Cleaning Company will be the name! Now, can you set up an email address and I will design some business cards?'

Lenny's mum worked hard and sent the finished design to the printers that afternoon.

The business cards arrived back a few days later and so Lenny and his mum started taking

them round to the local houses and flats, putting one in the post office window, a few in the local coffee shops and the launderette and one on the counter of the hardware store on the high street.

On the way home from school, Lenny's mum asked him to put a card through Mrs Portman's letterbox at the back of her house. He stood up tall and bravely walked up the long garden path. As he walked by the house he could see a dirty curtain move but he opened the letterbox anyway and pushed through the card. He turned and ran quickly back down the path (Lenny was brave, but he wasn't stupid!)

Chapter 4

Lenny went straight into his new little bedroom and shut the door. He managed to find his Lego and started to make his own version of the Eiffel Tower as they had been learning about Paris at school that day.

Half an hour later his mum knocked on the door. 'Lenny, I have had a call from Mrs Portman and she wants me to clean her home once a week!'

'Well, good luck with that!' was all he said and continued to make his rather magnificent version of the Eiffel Tower.

When he came out eventually for his tea he was amazed... all the packing boxes were gone and Mum had made half of the kitchen into a cosy sitting room. There was a beautiful throw over the old, saggy sofa in pink, orange and green and what looked like a very comfortable rug to sit on in the middle of the floor, in all sorts of colours. Mum told him that the rug was a 'rag rug', very popular in the Victorian era, about 150 years ago.

'Wow, Mum, good work!' said Lenny. 'Can I have my tea sitting on the rug? Err, what is for tea?'

It was fish fingers, beans and chips with yoghurt and bananas for pudding. Lenny thought that the fish fingers were a good idea but he wasn't too impressed with the pudding!

Lenny's mum then went over to the kitchen chair and picked up an apron with huge pockets across the front. Putting it on over her dungarees, she started to fill the pockets with cleaning materials; cream cleaner in one pocket, (environmentally friendly, of course), a short-handled window cleaner squeegee in another, a bottle of washing up liquid (again, kind to the planet), while another pocket was full of dusters. Over her shoulder, she placed a long-handled brush that was attached to a long strap.

'Mum, you are like the cleaning version of Mary Poppins!' exclaimed Lenny.

'I know, and I even bought a ribbon to hold this lot back,' and from her dungarees pocket, she pulled out a shiny red ribbon and fixed it around her long locks of hair.

'Ta da!' she shouted, with arms flung up like an actor accepting the audience's cheers, before giving a theatrical bow in front of Lenny.

Lenny clapped his hands gleefully.

The next morning when Lenny woke up, there was steaming porridge and orange juice waiting for him on the kitchen table and Mum was ready with his school bag and packed lunch.

'Come on, Lenny, we will be early for school. I am starting at Mrs Portman's house this morning.'

'Early for school, this was a first,' thought Lenny!

They got to school so early that Lenny had time to tell Jacob all about a new computer game that had just come out before the bell went and it was time to go in for registration.

Chapter 5

That evening Mum told Lenny about her first day cleaning for Mrs Portman.

'Lenny, she wasn't scary at all. She is just very lonely and she has arthritis so she is very stiff and finds getting about very difficult. She told me that she used to love keeping her home 'spick and span'; that means clean and tidy, but hasn't been able to do it for a very long time. But I have made a good start and her kitchen looks lovely now and I have washed her net curtains and cleaned the windows so she can look out and see the garden more easily.'

'To catch me swinging from her tree,' thought Lenny but he let Mum go on.

'Next to her kitchen she has the same little room that we made into your bedroom. Well, it's a real muddle; full of old boxes and pieces of old furniture and general rubbish! I was wondering whether you could come with me on Saturday to help clear it out for Mrs Portman?'

Lenny thought that didn't sound like fun and then he remembered that he had been invited to Jacob's house anyway.

'You could go a little later, Lenny,' said Mum. 'It won't take long if we start in the morning.'

The next day at school, Lenny asked Jacob if he could come later on Saturday and Jacob said that was a good idea as he could stay for tea instead, so on Saturday morning Lenny and his mum arrived bright and early at Mrs Portman's house...

Chapter 6

Although Lenny was very nervous about meeting Mrs Portman, he stood tall next to his mum. They knocked on the door and after what seemed like a very long time, Lenny heard the lock turn and a bolt on the other side of the door being pulled back. The door opened and a very smiley old lady, not as tall as Lenny, appeared.

'Hello, you two! So nice to meet you, Lenny, your mum has told me a lot about you.'

Lenny put his hand out and got such a firm handshake back from this tiny, frail-looking lady it quite surprised him. And she was so friendly! He almost wondered if she had a grumpy twin that he had seen knocking on the window the other day!

Mrs Portman showed them both through to her kitchen. It was lovely and clean; his mum had obviously worked her magic. It looked very old fashioned but beautiful with a large pale blue painted dresser, full of plates and cups hanging from the shelves.

'I think you are here to tidy my messy pantry,' said Mrs Portman to Lenny.

'Yes, but next door, this room is my bedroom!' he replied.

It was crammed with boxes and an ironing board hung on the door. Three rusty bicycles were pushed up against one wall and he couldn't even see the floor for buckets, tins of paint, old gardening tools and piles of newspapers and magazines.

'You have some work to do!' she laughed and then said she would put the kettle on.

Mum and Lenny spent the morning sorting out the pantry. They made different piles; stuff to go to the charity shop, stuff to keep and things that would need to go to the recycling centre. Just when Lenny was flagging and had started to wonder when he would be allowed to go to Jacob's house to play, his mum suddenly gave such a loud shriek he almost dropped the newspapers he had been carrying.

'A spider, Mum?'

Then he realized that his mum was looking down in a dark corner of the room at an old case. She picked it up and read out loud from a dusty old red label in the middle of it.

'Anna Carter. Is that you, Mrs Portman?'

'Yes, when I was a little girl during the war, me and my friends were sent to live with families in the countryside in Wales so we would be safe

27

from the bombs that were being dropped in London. That was the case I took for my evacuation. Have a look inside.'

When they opened it, they found a school beret and a maroon blazer with a badge saying St Williams on the front pocket. There were some exercise books and a jotter. There was also a ration book with her name written on it. She told them that during the war, food was scarce so was rationed so everyone would get some. Near the bottom of the case was a recipe book with 'Bero Flour' written on the front and inside it was dated, '1941 to Anna, love Mummy.'

'Yes, my mum gave it to me when I was evacuated so I could bake for the family I was staying with to say thank you. I was good at baking and do you know the thing that they liked me making most? Apple crumble!'

'Oh, that is my favourite pudding,' said Lenny, 'but Mum doesn't do much baking'.

He raised his eyes to his mum.

'No. I am not very good at it,' said Mum.

Mrs Portman smiled. 'Well, Lenny, why don't I teach you? Look by the door, there is a basket of cooking apples from the garden. I don't think you noticed my apple tree when you ran up the drive the other morning? Perhaps you were running too fast? Did I scare you the other day?'

Lenny nodded.

'Sorry, Lenny. Actually you gave me a fright; I thought someone was trying to climb into my garden! Why don't we make an apple crumble together tomorrow for your lovely, hardworking mum?'

Chapter 7

Following a brilliant evening with Jacob, including a marathon game of 'Hot Wheels', Lenny had got ready and was now standing at Mrs Portman's back door. After knocking a few times, increasing the banging (she must be pretty deaf, Lenny thought), she came to the door. As she opened it, he could feel the heat from her kitchen and the delicious smell of apples cooking.

'Hello, Lenny. Come in, come in!'

Following her, he saw clouds of flour falling off her apron as she walked leaving a little trail of

white dust behind her. The back door led straight into her huge kitchen. The lovely smell just got stronger and Lenny saw a large pan of bubbling apples on the stove with yet more apples in a basket, ready to be cut up on a large wooden board.

'So, Lenny, I will show you how to make the crumble and you will always have delicious puddings!'

Lenny washed his hands at the basin and dried them with a small towel, pushed up his sleeves and watched as Mrs Portman laid out bowls of butter, flour and sugar. She put a large bowl in front of

Lenny and as directed by Mrs Portman, he poured the flour into the bowl which was covered in a large sieve. Patting the edge of the sieve, the flour gently floated into the bowl. Pulling the large piece of butter into little chunks as she showed him with the tips of his fingers, he carefully combined the ingredients.

'It should start to become like soft, light breadcrumbs very quickly, Lenny.'

With his sleeves pulled right up, he flicked the mixture gently through his fingertips as it became lighter, fluffy and snow flakey - it felt lovely! Finally, he added the sugar.

But then Mrs Portman came over.

'My secret ingredient, to give it a bit of crunch,' as she poured on flaked oats.

Next, she brought over a very large container half-full of delicious, cooked apples and Lenny helped her hold the bowl as they poured in the crumbly mixture.

'Half an hour in the oven and it will be ready, Lenny.'

However, just like in the best children's programmes, she had prepared one earlier for him while he waited. Served with a delicious dollop of thick cream.

Lenny sat down with his spoon, cracked through the crispy, crumbly topping and took a large creamy mouthful.

'Wow!' he said. 'Amazing!'

The next day Mum put the huge tray of apple crumble into a flat-bottomed bag and Lenny took it into school. Miss Gentle was delighted and said at the first break they could all have some, so at eleven a.m. she produced bowls and spoons and the whole class sat down to sample the crumble. Everyone wanted more and Lenny was so happy.

He told the class about Mrs Portman and how scary she had been. Miss Gentle said that it reminded her of a story she read as a little girl called 'The Selfish Giant' by Oscar Wilde, who lived a very long time ago, but the story was still very good. She said that sometimes people feel lonely and forget how to chat and enjoy company and that it was lovely that Lenny's mum had been able to help.

That night when Lenny got to bed, he was thinking about his favourite Aunt Minnie, who was coming to stay in a few days' time. Lenny was so pleased because she was great fun. He found life hard without his lovely dad and missed him so much. It had been such a tough year with so many challenges to face, but lying there in his tiny bedroom with the painted beach scene as his window, he felt that the move to London, the new school and beginning to feel part of things wasn't

 so frightening after all, and he fell asleep.